Jonathan London

THE LION
WHO HAD ASTHMA

Pictures by **Nadine Bernard Westcott**

ALBERT WHITMAN & COMPANY
MORTON GROVE, ILLINOIS

For my son Sean
and every child who has ever had asthma,
and for my wife, Maureen Weisenberger,
the lion's mother, with love.
With thanks to
Paula Pearce, Director of Programs,
American Lung Association of the Redwood Empire,
and for Sean's pediatrician, Jeffrey Miller, M.D. *J.L.*

For Becky and Wendy. *N.B.W.*

A NOTE FOR PARENTS
OF CHILDREN WHO HAVE ASTHMA

When our son, the Sean (pronounced Shawn) of this story, had his first asthma attack as a baby, we had to rush him to an emergency room in the middle of the night. It was a distressing experience for all of us.

We soon learned much about asthma, a lung disease which causes breathing problems for almost ten million Americans. Around three million are children under the age of eighteen. It is the most common chronic disease of childhood.

There is no cure for asthma yet, but the symptoms, such as coughing and wheezing, can be controlled. And attacks, or "episodes," can be stopped once they have begun. There are various treatments for asthma, and they are aimed at preventing as well as stopping episodes.

Now four years old, Sean has his own nebulizer for use at home, and the experience is far more manageable. The nebulizer turns liquid medicine into a mist which is easy for him to inhale through a mask. Sean's nebulizer is the machine shown in this book; there are also several other types of nebulizers.

Sean's medicine, administered with the nebulizer, is a bronchodilator. It relaxes the muscles in the airway walls and helps open the airways.

Relaxes is a key word; relaxing makes being sick easier to bear and to control. Breathing exercises and visualization help lead to relaxation. Visualization is a product of the imagination, and like most young children, Sean has a great imagination. Encourage a child's imagination! It is not only an asset in the treatment of asthma but enhances life itself.

Jonathan London

Sean is a lion
roaring in the jungle.

Now he's a hippo
singing in the bathtub.

At suppertime,
he's a **G I A N T**
munching trees . . .
C-a-a-*runch!*

Now he's a lion again,
with awesome teeth
and fearsome claws.
Grrrrrrrrrrroww . . .

Cough, cough—

The lion has a cough.
His chest hurts,
and it's hard for him
to breathe.

The lion has asthma.

Instead of growling and roaring, he wheezes.
It sounds like there's a squeaky whistle
inside him when he breathes.

The lion feels tired
and a little bit frightened.
He feels like crying.

"It's time for your treatment,
Sean," says his mom.

Sean doesn't feel like being a lion anymore.
He curls up and cries
and coughs and coughs
and breathes faster and faster.

"Okay, Sean," says his mom.
"Quiet, now. Just breathe soft and easy.
Here's your mask. Time to be a pilot!"

Sean sits up and puts on his mask.
He says, "*I* want to turn it on!"

He presses the power switch,
and the machine starts up.
It's noisy, like a jet taking off.

In his mask,
Sean is a jet pilot
flying high in the sky.

The steam is the clouds.
The knobs are the controls.
Zoooooom! he goes, Jet Pilot Sean,
flying faster and faster,
higher and higher.

"Breathe deep, Jet Pilot Sean,"
says his dad,
with arms spread like wings.

Sean's chest doesn't hurt now.
His coughing has stopped,
and the wheezing sound, too.
He can *breathe!*

Sean stops flying
and comes down for a landing.

He's a lion again—
the King of the Jungle.

The illustrations are watercolor and ink.
The text typeface is Bookman Regular.

Library of Congress Cataloging-in-Publication Data

London, Jonathan, 1947—
The lion who had asthma / Jonathan London;
illustrated by Nadine Bernard Westcott.
p.   c.m.
Summary: Sean's nebulizer mask and his imagination aid in his recov-
ery following an asthma attack. Includes information on childhood
asthma and how to control its symptoms.
ISBN 0-8075-4559-7 (hardcover)
ISBN 0-8075-4560-0 (paperback)
[1. Asthma—Fiction. 2. Imagination—Fiction.]
I. Westcott, Nadine Bernard, ill. II. Title.
PZ7.L8432Li   1992   91-16553
[E]—dc20   CIP
                                            AC

ABOUT THE AUTHOR

Jonathan London's poetry and short stories have appeared in over one hundred magazines. This is his second book for children. Jonathan lives in Graton, California, with his wife, Maureen, and their sons, Sean and Aaron. He has traveled all over the world and, when not writing, loves to kayak, hike, dance, and read. He has held a variety of jobs, among them dancer, cannery worker, laborer, landscaper, bookstore clerk, counselor at a juvenile home, display installer at trade shows, and poet in the schools.

ABOUT THE ARTIST

Nadine Bernard Westcott began her art career as a greeting card designer for Hallmark Cards in Kansas City. After moving to Vermont, she married her husband, Bill, and in 1980 they founded their own greeting card company, Hartland Cards. Her work creating humorous cards led Nadine to publish her first children's book in 1980. Since then, she has written and illustrated or illustrated more than fifteen books for children, among them *Even Little Kids Get Diabetes*.

Nadine lives in Woodstock, Vermont, with her husband and their daughters, Becky and Wendy. The family spends summers on the island of Nantucket.